The Empty Doll's House

Sally has no furniture to put inside her empty doll's house. She wants to get some straight away, but before she does, she must learn to be patient.

Enid Blyton's

The Empty Doll's House

illustrated by Edgar Hodges

Copyright © 1990 by Darrell Waters Limited and
World International Publishing Limited. All rights reserved.
Published in Great Britain by World International Publishing Limited,
An Egmont Company,
Egmont House, P.O.Box 111 Great Ducie Street, Manchester M60 3BL.
Printed in DDR. ISBN 0 7235 4451 4

A CIP catalogue record for this book is available from the British Library.

Sally had a lovely little doll's house on Christmas Day. She looked at it standing there at the foot of her bed. It had a blue front door with a knocker that really knocked, and it had four small windows, with lace curtains!

"Oh, it's lovely!" said Sally. "Won't my Belinda Jane love to live there! She is small enough to fit it properly."

But when she opened the front of the doll's house, Sally got a shock. It was empty. There was no furniture at all!

She was disappointed. A doll's house can't be played with unless it has furniture inside, and Sally wanted to play with it.

Also, Belinda Jane couldn't possibly live
there if it was empty. She must at least have a
bed, a chair and a table to have meals on.

Sally showed the house to Belinda Jane.
Belinda looked sad when she saw it was empty.

"Never mind. I'll save up my money and buy some furniture," said Sally. "Maybe I'll get some money for a present."

But she didn't. All her aunts and uncles gave her Christmas presents of toys and books, and nobody gave her money at all.

It was Granny who had given her the doll's house. When she came to eat Christmas dinner she spoke to Sally about the house. "I didn't put any furniture in it, dear," she said. "I thought you would find it more fun to buy some yourself and furnish it bit by bit."

"Yes it *will* be fun to do that," said Sally. "Only it will take such a long time, Granny, because I spent all my money on Christmas presents, and I only get fifty pence a week."

When Sally got her first fifty pence she went to the toyshop and looked at the doll's furniture.

She saw a cardboard box and in it was a
dear little bed, two chairs, a table and a
wardrobe! Think of that!

But, oh dear, it cost three pounds, and there
was nothing at all that fifty pence would buy!
Sally was almost in tears!

"Now don't be a baby," said Mummy. "Everything comes to those who wait patiently. Don't get cross and upset if you can't have what you want. It will come!"

Sally was not a very patient person, and she hated waiting for things she really wanted. But she always believed what Mummy said, so she told Belinda Jane they must both be patient, and maybe they would get the furniture somehow in the end.

Sally was excited next day, she was going to a party – and there was to be a Christmas tree. It was sure to be a nice big one, with a present for everyone. And there would be games and crackers and ice-creams. Lovely!

She went to the party in her best blue frock.

"Hello, Sally!" cried Eileen, dancing up to her. "There's going to be a prize for every game, did you know? And it's to be money! I hope I win a prize, it's Mum's birthday next week and I want to buy her some flowers."

Sally was pleased about the prizes. If only she could win some of the money! She would be able to buy some furniture for Belinda Jane.

They played musical chairs. Sally didn't win because a little boy pushed her out of her chair, and she didn't like to push back.

They played hunt the thimble, but Sally could never see the thimble first! So she didn't win a prize at all.

"Now, I mustn't get cross or upset," Sally said to herself. "I must be patient. But I've missed my chance. What a pity!"

After tea the children were taken into another room – and there was the Christmas tree, reaching up to the ceiling, hung with presents from top to bottom.

Just about the middle of the tree there hung a cardboard box. The box of furniture Sally had seen in the toyshop! Her heart jumped for joy. Now surely her patience would have its reward. Surely, she would get that lovely box of doll's furniture!

Sally could hardly wait for the presents to be given out. She had good manners, so she didn't like to ask for the box of furniture. She just stood near by, hoping it would be hers.

But to her disappointment, it wasn't given to her! She was handed a box of tiny motor cars instead. Sally could have cried! But she said thank you and went to a corner, trying not to feel upset.

"I wanted to win a prize and I didn't. I wanted to have the furniture off the tree and I didn't," she thought. "What's the good of being patient? I don't get what I want however patient I am. I feel like shouting and stamping!"

But Sally didn't shout or stamp, because she knew better. She just sat and looked at the little motor cars, and didn't like them a bit.

A girl called Fanny came up to her. She held the box of furniture in her hand. She sat down beside Sally and looked at the motor cars. "Oh, aren't they lovely?" she said. "I do like them. I got this doll's furniture. Look, isn't it silly?"

"Well, I think it's lovely," said Sally. "How *can* you think it's silly?"

"It's silly for me, because I haven't got a doll's house," said Fanny. "But I *have* got a toy garage! I had it for Christmas. It's only got one car, and I do want some more. That's why I like your present and hate mine!"

"I had a doll's house for Christmas, without any furniture, and I haven't got a garage!" said Sally. "Can't you give me the furniture and I'll give you the motor cars? We could ask Eileen's mum and see if she minds. She bought all the presents for us."

They ran to Eileen's mum and asked her. She smiled at them. "Of course, change your presents if you want to," she said. "I think it would be most sensible. I would have given *you* the furniture, Sally, and *you* the cars, Fanny, if I'd known about the doll's house and the garage."

The little girls were so pleased. Fanny took the cars home to her toy garage and Sally raced home with her doll's furniture. It went into the doll's house and looked beautiful!

"There you are, Belinda Jane," said Sally. "Now you can move in. You've got a bed, some chairs, a wardrobe for your clothes and a table to have meals on. I'll buy you a little cooker as soon as I can."

Belinda Jane was pleased. She looked sweet, sitting on one of the chairs, and even sweeter tucked up in the little bed.

Mummy came to look. Sally gave her a great big hug.

"Mummy, you were right about waiting patiently. I kept on being disappointed, but I wouldn't get cross or upset. Then suddenly the furniture just came to me. Wasn't it lucky?"

"It was," said Mummy. "Tomorrow I'll give you some bits and pieces and you can make carpets for Belinda Jane. She will like that."

You should see Sally's doll's house now. She saved up her money and bought a little lamp, a cooker, another bed, a cupboard for the kitchen, two more chairs and a washstand. I really wouldn't mind living in that doll's house myself.